INSECTO
INVASION

Written by Anna Nilsen   Illustrated by Philip Nicholson

DERSLEY

ART • MOSCOW • SYDNEY

.dk.com

THE STORY SO FAR – THE ZOTAXIANS INVADE

After a fight with their cruel leader, the Zotaxians fled from Planet Zotax and searched for a better place to live. They crash-landed on a rough, barren planet called Holox. There they set up a base station.

However, the base station soon began to fail. The planet's rocky surface

Zotaxian

did not have any of the essential life force that the Zotaxians' plants needed. Then, when all seemed lost, they began drilling into Holox's surface to try and find some new energy sources. Inside the planet they discovered another *amazing world* with its own sun!

20114
793.73

The Inner World

They were not alone! This Inner World was inhabited by ferocious creatures called Bilgin Bugs. Its sun provided life-giving energy for

Bilgin Bug

the eggs laid by the Bugs. The Zotaxians realised that they too could use this life-

Bilgin Bug egg

Voltstone

giving energy. So they made voltstones that looked like the Bugs' eggs. These yellow voltstones can absorb and store the inner sun's energy for later use.

The Zotaxians then disguised six of their space cruisers as Bugs. The cruisers are called **Insectoids**.

Insectoid

The Insectoids travel through the deep holes drilled in the planet's crust. They follow routes marked out by symbols. Once in the Inner World, the Insectoids plant the voltstones to absorb the inner sun's energy. When the voltstones are charged, the Insectoids collect them and take them back to their Power House on the surface.

The Bugs Fight Back

The Bugs have realised that the invaders are robbing them of their vital energy and, worse still, destroying their eggs. The six most ferocious Bugs are set to guard the egg crop and to detect and destroy the voltstones. A titanic battle of survival begins that will have only one victor ...

Read the rules for navigating the planet (on pages 4 and 5) before attempting your first mission.

ZOTAXIAN MISSIONS

You are the Zotaxian commander. You must make sure the Zotaxians survive and rule the planet.

Start from the Power House on the planet's surface (page 6). One at a time, guide your six Insectoids to the dangerous Inner World and back. See the hazard box (below).

Power House
contains six
Insectoids

Mission Z1
Aim: Collect as many *yellow* voltstones from the Inner World as you can find *right by the trail*. If an Insectoid returns to the number of the Power House it started from, double its score.

Score less than 25 voltstones: you have failed! The Zotaxians are dying out. Try again.
Score 25-50: well done! The Zotaxians survive.
Score 51+: excellent! you're on the next mission.

Mission Z2
Aim: Destroy as many *green* Bug eggs as you can find. If an Insectoid returns to the number of the Power House it started from, double its score.

Score less than 25 eggs: the Bilgin Bug population is growing! Try again.
Score 25-50: well done! The Bugs are dying out.
Score 51+: excellent! You go on the next mission.

Mission Z3
Aim: To rule the planet! Guide your Insectoids to the Inner World and destroy any Bugs *whose wings touch the trail*. If an Insectoid returns to the number of the Power House it started from, double its score.

Score less than 14 Bugs destroyed: try again.
Score 14-25 destroyed: *you control Planet Holox!*

BILGIN BUG MISSIONS

You are King of the Bilgin Bugs. You want to eradicate the Zotaxians who have invaded *your* world. You must rule all Planet Holox!

Start from the Bug Dome in the Glass Barrier (page 12). You must guide your six Bugs, one by one, to the dangerous Inner World and back to the Dome. Beware the Ice Zone – it is fatal for Bugs! Check the hazard box (below).

Bug Dome
contains six
ferocious Bugs

Mission B1
Aim: Collect as many *green* Bug eggs from the Inner World as you can find *right by the trail*.

Score less than 25 eggs: your Bugs are dying out! Try again.
Score 25-50: the Bugs are fighting on.
Score 51+: great! You qualify for the next mission.

Mission B2
Aim: Destroy as many *yellow* voltstones as you can find.

Score less than 25 voltstones: the Zotaxian invaders are getting more powerful! Try again.
Score 25-50: you have weakened the Zotaxian colony. Well done.
Score 51+: you qualify for the next mission.

Mission B3
Aim: To destroy as many Insectoids as you can find touching the trail.

Score less than 14 Insectoids destroyed: try again.
Score 14-25 destroyed: *you control Planet Holox!*

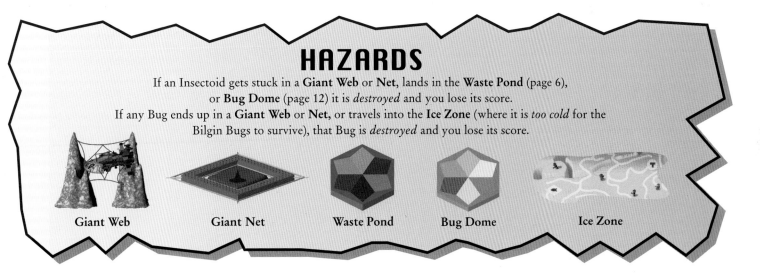

HAZARDS
If an Insectoid gets stuck in a **Giant Web** or **Net**, lands in the **Waste Pond** (page 6),
or **Bug Dome** (page 12) it is *destroyed* and you lose its score.
If any Bug ends up in a **Giant Web** or **Net,** or travels into the **Ice Zone** (where it is *too cold* for the
Bilgin Bugs to survive), that Bug is *destroyed* and you lose its score.

Giant Web   Giant Net   Waste Pond   Bug Dome   Ice Zone

NAVIGATING THROUGH THE PLANET

You will need a pencil and paper for recording scores.

1 Start at 1 in the Power House, for Zotaxian missions, or 1 in the Bug Dome, for Bilgin Bug missions. Follow the trail until you come to a round *Launch Pad*. Look at the symbol on it.

2 Take off. Fly until you find a diamond-shaped *Landing Pad* with the same symbol. Now follow the trail. When you come to a *hole* go through to the page beneath.

3 Leave the bottom of the hole on the *same side and colour* as you enter. Follow the trails and go down holes, until you reach the Lizards' Lair, at the very edge of the Inner World.

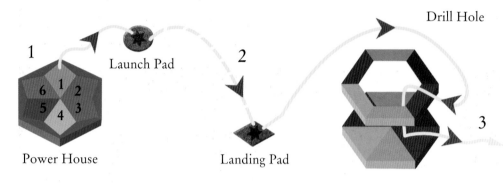

Once you have set off, don't turn back unless you come to a dead end, or a loop allows you to.

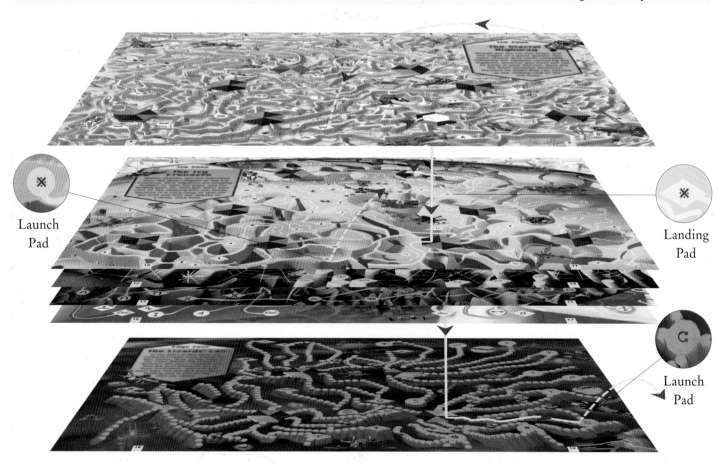

When you reach the Lizards' Lair (pages 18-19), the trail will take you to a symbol on a turquoise *Launch Pad*. Take off and go through the pages to a diamond-shaped *Landing Pad* in the Inner World.

Scoring In The Inner World

4 This is the critical part of your mission. Each time you pass a voltstone or Bug egg add *one* to your score. Keep travelling through the Inner World until you land on a circular turquoise Launch Pad – it will transport you to the *Lizards' Lair*, from where you must make your way home. As each Insectoid or Bug returns successfully to its base, or dies, the next one sets off on its mission.

5 From this Landing Pad, follow the trail. Within each level of the Inner World, you take off and land on matching Launch and Landing Pads as before. Don't forget, if a Bug or Insectoid ends up in a hazard, it is destroyed, and you lose its score.

6 Bright turquoise Launch Pads lead back to Landing Pads in the Lizards' Lair (pages 18-19). Once at the Lizards' Lair, each Bug or Insectoid can follow a symbol trail back to its base to complete its mission – if it survives!

7 Alternatively, you may come to a symbol in the bottom right-hand corner of the page. It will lead you deeper into the Inner World, where you can keep on adding to your score! Take off from this Launch Pad. You will find the matching Landing Pad on the very next page.

The Outer World

The Planet Holox

On the barren surface of the planet the Zotaxians cannot survive long without power.

• Insectoids start their journey here! Start from 1, following the symbols and going down holes.

• Don't pass the red-hot rocks.

• On your return, if you end on the number you started from, double your score.

• Land in the Waste Pond and you die!

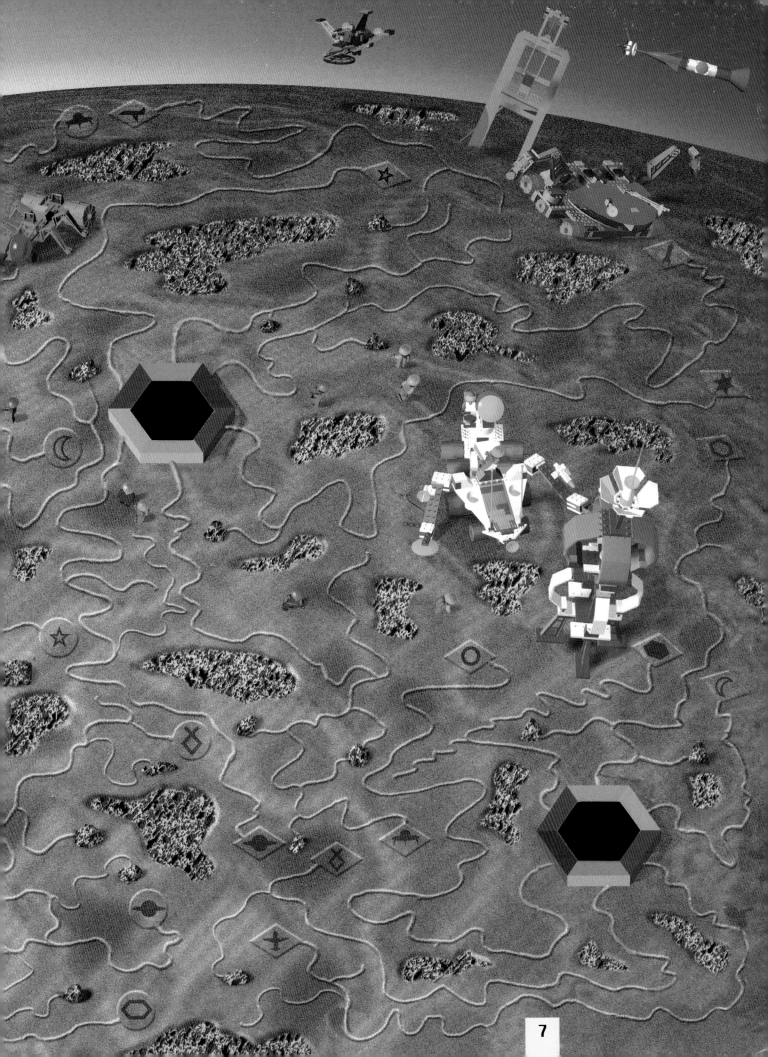

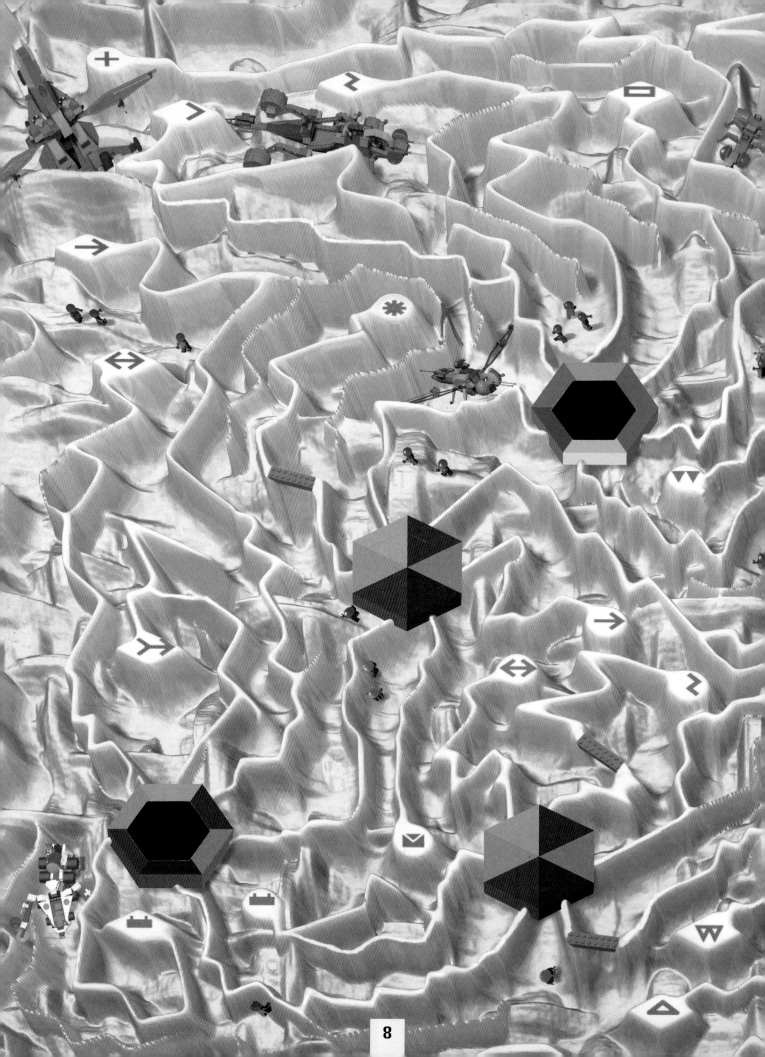

Ice Zone

The Glacial Highway

Beneath the surface lies a world of creaking glaciers. Don't fall when you cross the bridges.

- Choose your route, following the symbols carved in the ice.
- No Bilgin Bug can survive in the chilling cold of the Ice Zone.
- Remember — hurry to the Inner World to start scoring — time is short!

Ice Zone

The Icy Crevasse

Deep, grim crevasses wait to swallow the unwary — take care!

• Here in the Ice Zone Bilgin Bugs die in the cold — and lose all the eggs saved from the Inner World.

• Insectoids must hurry to the Inner World so they can start scoring — there are no voltstones here!

Web Zone

The Glass Barrier

Beware the massive spider's jaws!

- Bugs start missions here — from 1 on the Bug Dome — and must try to return home safely from the Inner World.
- Bugs that land on the number they started from double their score.
- Insectoids that land in the Bug Dome die and lose their scores.
- You cannot pass the sticky red blobs.

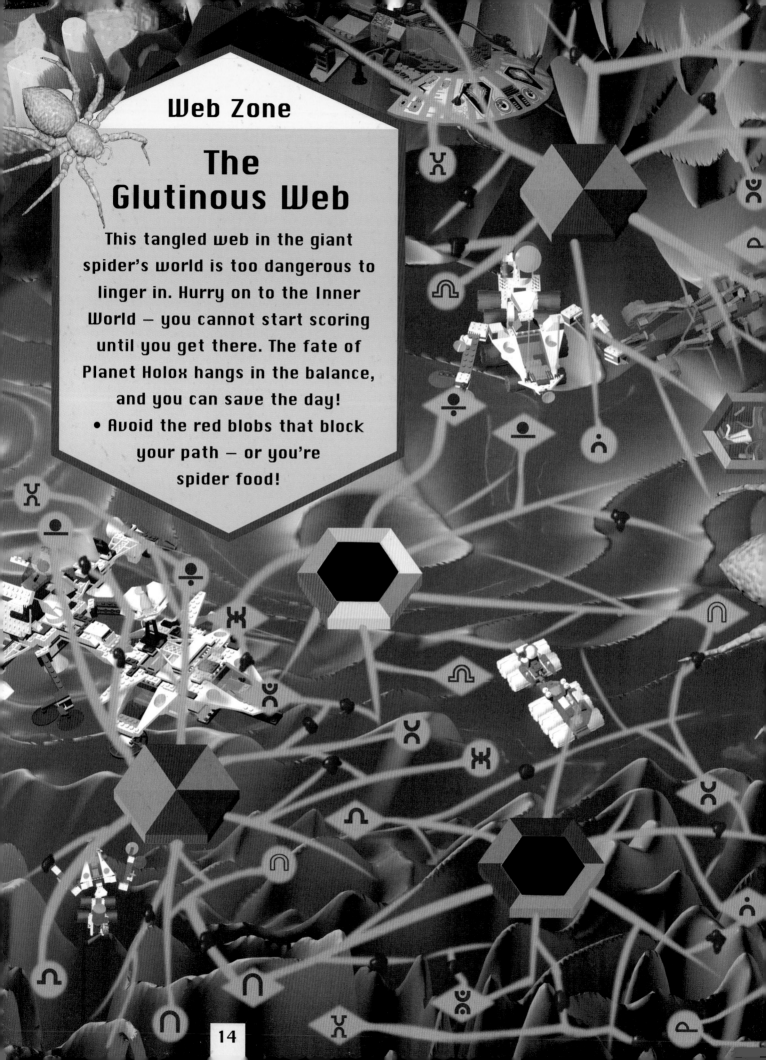

Web Zone

The Glutinous Web

This tangled web in the giant spider's world is too dangerous to linger in. Hurry on to the Inner World — you cannot start scoring until you get there. The fate of Planet Holox hangs in the balance, and you can save the day!

• Avoid the red blobs that block your path — or you're spider food!

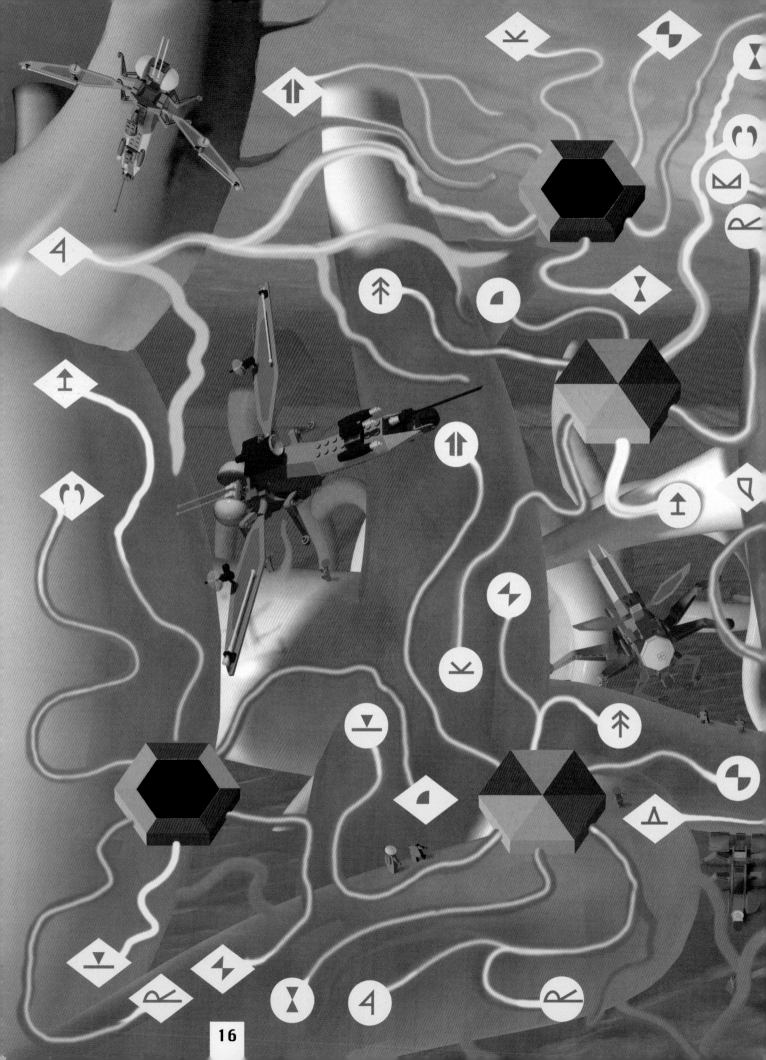

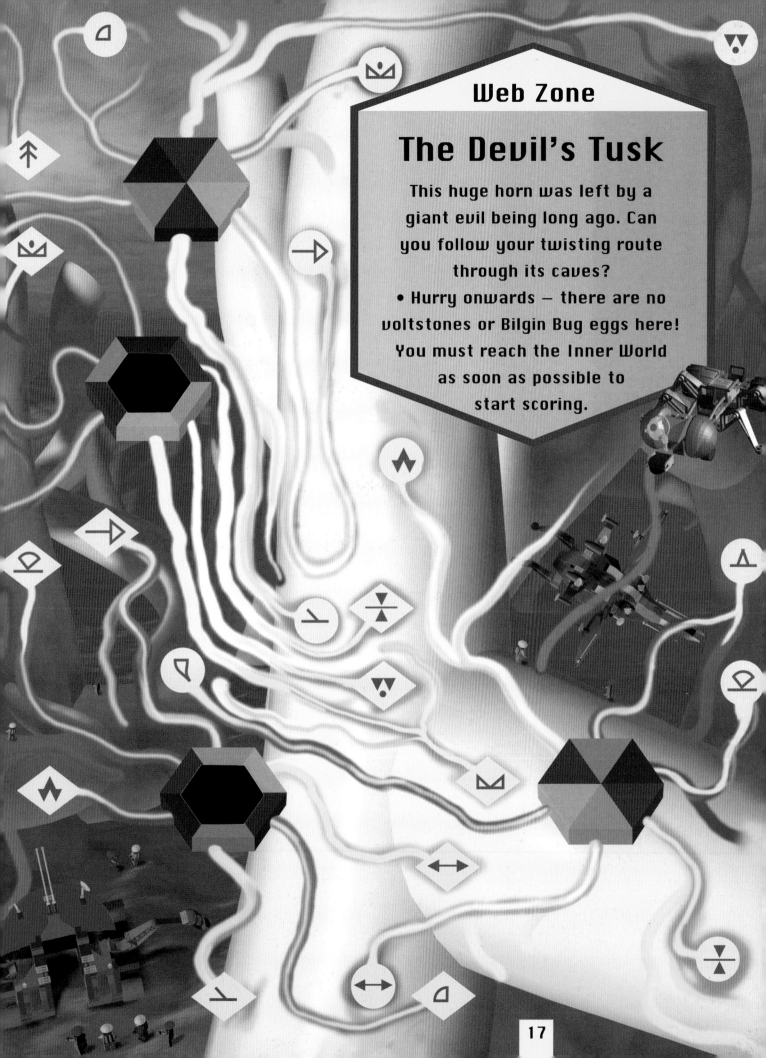

Web Zone

The Devil's Tusk

This huge horn was left by a giant evil being long ago. Can you follow your twisting route through its caves?

• Hurry onwards — there are no voltstones or Bilgin Bug eggs here! You must reach the Inner World as soon as possible to start scoring.

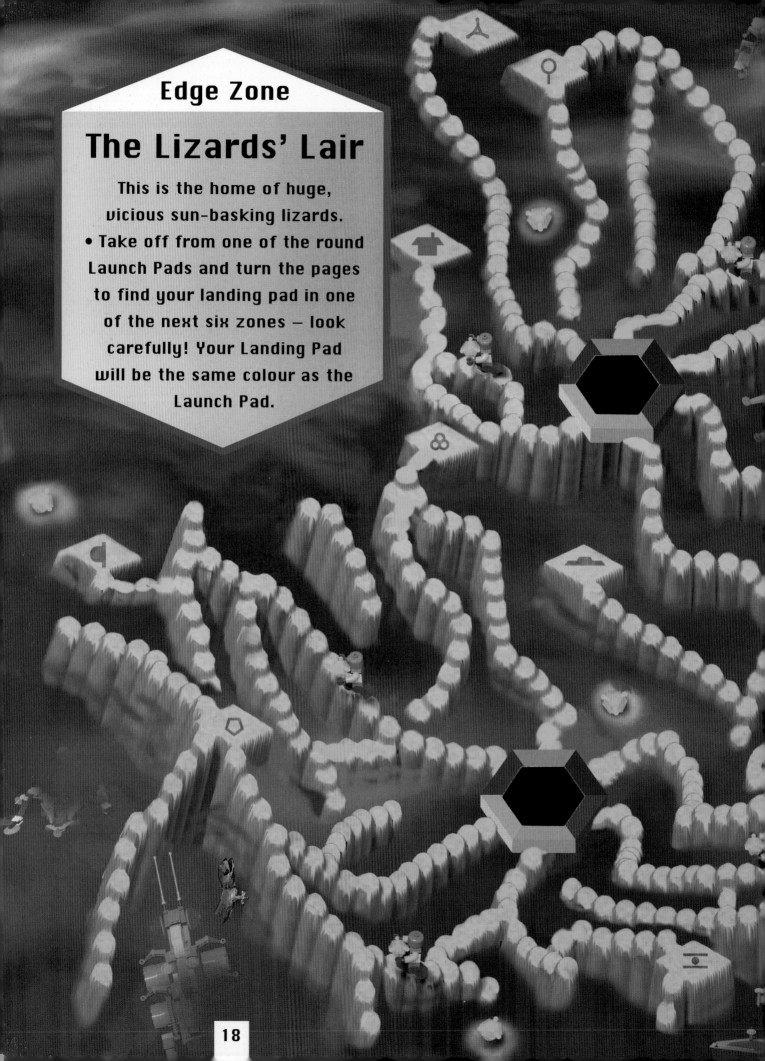

Edge Zone

The Lizards' Lair

This is the home of huge, vicious sun-basking lizards.

• Take off from one of the round Launch Pads and turn the pages to find your landing pad in one of the next six zones — look carefully! Your Landing Pad will be the same colour as the Launch Pad.

Inner World

2014
793.73

The Fossil Forest

This ghostly forest hides many secret graves of lost travellers.

• Start scoring now! Count one for each yellow voltstone or green egg found.

• If you land on a turquoise Launch Pad go back to the Lizards' Lair.

• If you arrive on the Launch Pad in the bottom right corner, turn the page to find your next Landing Pad.

Inner World

The Steaming Swamp

Don't drown or be eaten by Aquasharks in the swamp!

• Start scoring now! Count one for each yellow voltstone or green egg found, and count only those that lie right by the trail.

• If you land on a turquoise Launch Pad go back to the Lizards' Lair.

• If you arrive on the Launch Pad in the bottom right corner, turn the page.

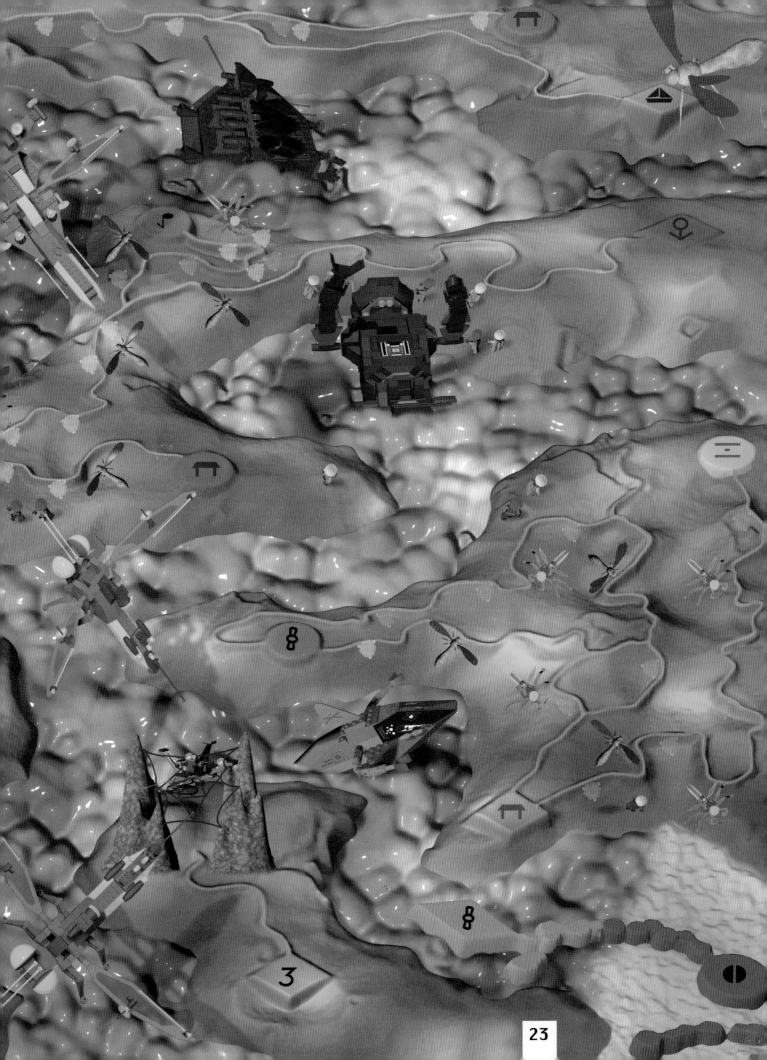

Inner World

The Golden River

Beware the molten lava that surges round the stepping stones.

• Start scoring now! Count one for each yellow voltstone or green egg found, and count only those that lie right by the trail.

• If you land on a turquoise Launch Pad go back to the Lizards' Lair.

• If you arrive on the Launch Pad in the bottom right corner, turn the page.

Inner World

The Valley of Venomous Vents

Beware of the toxic gases!

• Start scoring now! Count one for each yellow voltstone or green egg found, and count only those that lie right by the trail.

• If you land on a turquoise Launch Pad, go back to the Lizards' Lair.

• If you arrive on the Launch Pad in the bottom right corner, turn the page to find your Landing Pad.

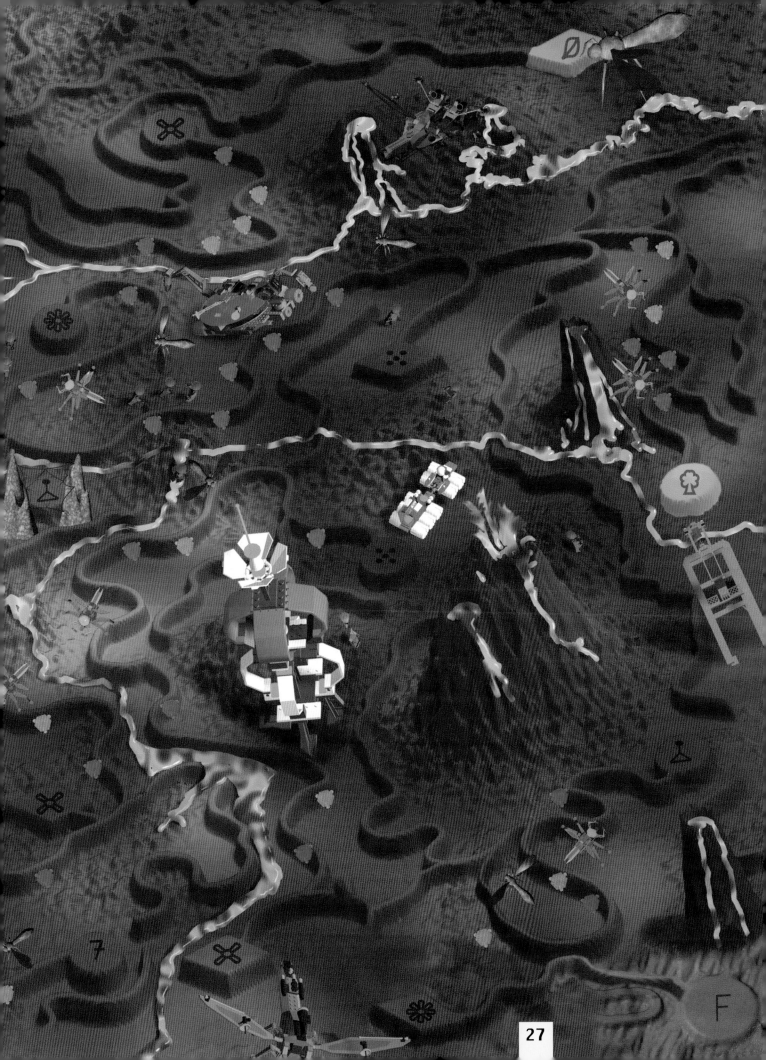

The Fermenting Vats

Here the Bugs mix a lethal broth made from fruits rotting in the sun.

• Start scoring now! Count one for each yellow voltstone or green egg found, and count only those that lie right by the trail.

• If you land on a turquoise Launch Pad go back to the Lizards' Lair.

• If you arrive on the Launch Pad in the bottom right corner, turn the page.

The Planet's Heart

The Flaming Furnace

This is the planet's fiery heart, close to the heat of the inner sun.

• Start scoring now! Count one for each yellow voltstone or green egg found, and count only those that lie right by the trail.

• When you land on a turquoise Launch Pad go back to the Lizards' Lair.

Some Insectoid Craft

These Insectoid craft have been altered by the Zotaxians to look like insects. Their flight across space taught them to be resourceful and determined – skills that they have used in disguising their cruisers. All the Insectoids have special roles, from scout craft to base vehicles. They collect and store voltstones, and attack the marauding Bilgin Bugs.

Collected voltstone on scout craft

Mosquito scout

This nippy little vehicle is great for getting about the planet undetected!

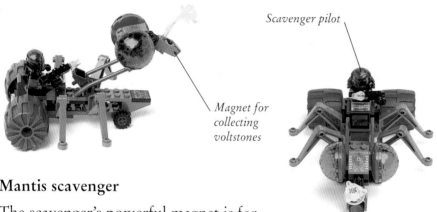

Scavenger pilot

Magnet for collecting voltstones

Mantis scavenger

The scavenger's powerful magnet is for collecting voltstones. Large rear wheels provide traction on rough ground.

Space swarm pod craft

Space swarm

Space swarms are the most common Insectoid vehicles – long-range cruisers with powerful armament. The front detaches to become a separate craft for short-range, high-speed missions that the larger Insectoid could not manage. Voltstones are collected by small and zippy pod craft with the capability to lift one voltstone at a time.

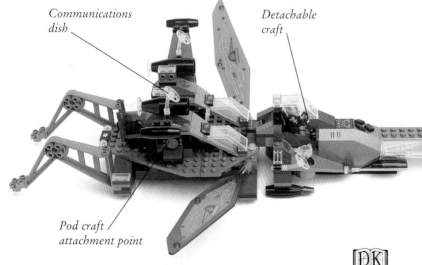

Communications dish

Detachable craft

Pod craft attachment point

DK

A DORLING KINDERSLEY BOOK

Visit us at www.dk.com

Managing Art Editor: Cathy Tincknell **Editors:** David Pickering and Nick Turpin
Designer: Nick Avery **DTP Designer:** Kim Browne

First published in Great Britain in 1998 by Dorling Kindersley Limited, 9 Henrietta Street, London WC2E 8PS

©1998 LEGO Group   ® LEGO is a Registered Trade Mark used here by special permission.

ISBN 1-86208-716-4

Colour reproduction by Imago Insite Plc   Printed in Hong Kong by Wing King Tong Co Ltd